Wizarding Wonder

FRED

Wizarding Wonder

SIMON PHILIP

Illustrated by SHEENA DEMPSEY

SIMON & SCHUSTER

First published in Great Britain in 2021 by Simon & Schuster UK Ltd

1 3 5 7 9 10 8 6 4 2

Simon & Schuster UK Ltd
1st Floor, 222 Gray's Inn Road
London
WC1X 8HB

www.simonandschuster.co.uk

Simon & Schuster Australia, Sydney
Simon & Schuster India, New Delhi

A CIP catalogue record for this book is available from the British
Library.

PB ISBN 978-1-4711-6912-0
eBook ISBN 978-1-4711-6913-7

Printed and bound by CPI Group (UK) Ltd, Croydon, CR0 4YY

MIX
Paper from
responsible sources
FSC® C020471

For Sylvia, Elsa, Juno,
Amelie, Belle and Seb –
with lots of love x

Chapter One

This is a story about Fred.

Now, Fred looked like any other ordinary boy. He had two eyes, a nose and a mouth on his face, and on each side of his head was a small, fleshy ear. As you'll know, these features are common. Rarely does a young boy have more or less than two ears, although sometimes you do hear about it. But only if you have ears yourself. If you don't have any, you won't hear a thing.

Like many boys, Fred liked pie. I don't mean the sixteenth letter of the Greek alphabet, or the numerical value of the ratio of the circumference of a circle to its diameter. Fred was too young to care about either of those, and I suspect you are too. No, I mean good old-fashioned pastry filled with things.

Fred also liked mash.

And what Fred really, *really* liked was pie *and* mash.

If you're wondering how to make pie and mash, it's simple. For the pie, wrap some pastry around something you fancy eating, and stick it in the oven. For the mash, boil some potatoes then mash them up. Use a masher. A hammer. Your neighbour's clogs. It doesn't matter. The important thing is that the potatoes end up *mashed*.

If you are going to combine pie with mash, make sure you choose the pie carefully. Lemon meringue pie tastes delicious on its own – but not so good with potatoes. Fred learned that the hard way.

Anyway, Fred still sounds pretty ordinary, doesn't he?

Well, he wasn't ...

Because Fred was a wizard.

Until recently, though, he was a wizard who was useless at magic. Fred had always been the odd one out in his family – a disappointment to his parents and siblings. But that was before he entered a competition to capture the tail of a terrifying fire-breathing lizard (named Linda) – which somehow, to everyone's surprise, including his own, he'd won!

His prize was a magic lesson with world-renowned wizard Merlin, which helped Fred unlock his magical ability and also turned out to be the start of a firm friendship. Just last month, Fred and his best friend, Marvin, had rescued Merlin from the evil wizard, Alan Kazam.

So, after two dangerous adventures in as many months, Fred was happy to be drama-free for a while. For the first time in ages, he felt settled and worry-free. Thanks to his lessons with Merlin, he felt more confident than ever about his magic, which seemed to be – by Fred's standards – unusually reliable. At school, he was finally keeping up with his classmates. He no longer embarrassed himself by making a mess of the simplest spells. He'd even started to find school *enjoyable*. Everything was falling into place.

But all that was about to change, because one normal Monday morning, just as he was about to leave for school, the arrival of a package through his bedroom window left Fred feeling distinctly unsettled.

Another adventure had just begun – whether he liked it or not.

Chapter Two

'Fred! Over here!'

The call woke Fred from his dazed amble towards the school entrance. He couldn't stop thinking about the strange package and what it meant. He followed his best friend's shouts across the playground. Marvin seemed ready to burst with excitement.

'I've been waiting for ages! What took you so long?'

'Sorry, I had a strange start to the—' Fred began, before Marvin interrupted.

'Never mind – I've got something incredible to show you!'

Marvin grinned as he waved an official-looking letter and a photo of what appeared to be an enormous, unusual building.

'I finally got one! An invitation to M.A.G.I.C. Camp! I've always wanted to go – my parents both went, and say it's amazing – but you can't apply, you have to be invited – the people in charge must have learned about what I can do from the news of our adventure. I *bet* that's why! They think I'm a magician of astounding genius, intrepidness and courage – that's what M.A.G.I.C. stands for, after all!'

Fred couldn't get a word in.

'*AND* I get to miss some school! It's fine –
Mum and Dad have already said I can go,

and schools are told automatically when the invitations get sent out. Fred, I'm going to learn *so* much! Every famous and important wizard and witch was helped on their way by M.A.G.I.C. Camp – the Prime Minister for Magic; Leroy Looney, the first wizard to fly to the moon on a broomstick ... And the M.A.G.I.C. Medal you get if you complete it is a really big deal – Dad said it's impossible to work for U.N.I.C.O.R.N. without one, as well as loads of other cool jobs. But, best of all, it means you're able to attend M.A.G.I.C. *School* – where you learn *literally* everything – INSTEAD OF BORING REGULAR SCHOOL! How AWESOME is that? Oh, I can't wait!'

Marvin stopped to catch his breath.

'That's brilliant, Marv – and it's about time! I'm really happy for you. You so deserve it!' Fred said, smiling. He knew how much this meant to his friend.

'Thanks, Fred. I just hope I actually make it there.'

'What do you mean?'

'That's the first challenge. They don't give you the address, just a vague location and a photo of the campus. Apparently, five attempts is all you get. Any more and their magic sends you home.'

Fred knew all too well how difficult travelling by click could be. It was only after he'd won the lizard competition that he'd first managed to 'click-and-go', which was how most wizards and witches travelled. Until then, he'd travelled by bus. He doubted there was a service that went to wherever M.A.G.I.C. Camp was.

'Well, I'm sure you'll manage, Marv. By the way, did your invitation come through your bedroom window, even though it was closed?'

Marvin looked shocked. 'How did you know that?'

Fred kept his face straight. 'Because that's how mine arrived.'

'Wait!' Marvin raised his eyebrows.

again right now, Marv.'

Marvin nodded. 'Consider where you'd be if you'd never left it, though.'

Marvin had a point. If Fred was honest with himself, he knew his life was significantly better because he'd challenged himself, that he'd almost certainly still be useless at magic and feeling like an embarrassment to everyone had he not. But before his first adventure, he'd had nothing to lose. Now, there was much more at risk.

Marvin interrupted Fred's contemplation.

'It's up to you. But you'd better decide quickly.' The bell rang for the start of school and the boys headed inside. 'Our invitations expire tomorrow, and if you're not at camp by then, you've *no* chance of getting there.'

'You got one too?'

Fred pulled his invitation fro
rucksack.

'Oh. Well, that's … *great*. Well done.

'I guess,' Fred said, a little disappoir
by Marvin's reaction. He'd hoped his b
friend would show more excitement at th
news, at the chance of sharing anothei
exciting experience. 'Thanks.'

'Are you going to come?' Marvin's tone
made Fred wonder what answer Marvin
wanted him to give.

'I guess so, it's just … well … I'm not
a great wizard like you are, and I doubt I
could keep up … whereas at school I *finally*
fit in. I'm enjoying feeling settled for once.
I'm not sure I want to leave my comfort zone

Chapter Three

When Fred arrived home after school, he still hadn't decided what to do about M.A.G.I.C. Camp. The more he thought about things, the more puzzling they seemed.

He supposed he'd been invited for the same reason Marvin had: his role in helping Marvin's parents and their U.N.I.C.O.R.N. (Universal Network Investigating Crimes of Remarkable Nastiness) colleagues capture

Alan Kazam, rescue Merlin and return *The Tome* to the museum. But M.A.G.I.C. Camp was for wizards and witches of 'astounding genius'. Marvin had performed plenty of impressive magic during their adventure. Fred, though? He'd just read books, asked questions and thought a lot.

As for intrepidness and courage, he'd simply used his common sense and determination. He'd been far from fearless.

He knew his magic was maybe a smidgeon above average for wizards his age on a good day, but he was no match for Marvin. If everyone at camp were as good as or better than Marvin, he could already feel how out of place he'd be. And experience had taught him that pressure had a terrible effect on his magic. What if it deserted him again, only this time so badly that he couldn't get it back? And that was if he even managed to get there. He tried not to dwell on the thought of becoming trapped, mid-click-and-go, in some sort of limbo-land, unable to find either M.A.G.I.C. Camp or his way home …

Marvin's reaction to Fred's invitation was bothering him too. It had been unexpectedly … *underwhelming*. Although maybe that was because attending M.A.G.I.C. Camp was *Marvin's* dream, not his own.

'So, Marvin got an invitation to M.A.G.I.C. Camp today,' Fred announced at the dinner table, as enchanted spoons served the food. His twin brothers, Wolf and

Wilbert, had also bewitched their cutlery to transport food from their plates to their mouths, so they need not move their arms. It was a strange sight: they sat opening and closing their mouths like fish in a pond.

'That's fabulous news!' Fred's parents smiled. 'About time, don't you think?' his dad added. 'Marvin's always been M.A.G.I.C. Camp material.'

'Lucky!' Wolf rolled his eyes. 'It's meant to be amazing! I've heard you get to do loads of stuff you wouldn't at school, and the

teachers' magic is incredible!'

'Me too,' Wilbert sang. 'I've heard the opening ceremony is *unbelievable*! And apparently the setting is home to loads of magical creatures which the students get to meet.'

The twins suddenly looked a bit sad.

'I can't believe we've never been invited,' Wilbert announced.

'I know. We meet all the criteria.' Wolf nodded. 'We're intrepid and courageous geniuses!'

'Fearless, brave, abnormally intelligent ...'

'And *exceptionally* modest,' Willow, one of Fred's sisters, said sarcastically. 'You must be excited for him, Fred?'

'Of course.' Fred paused. 'But I can't decide if I should go too.'

The twins snorted with laughter.

'You can't just *choose* to go!' Wilbert chuckled.

Wolf spoke extra slowly, as if Fred was mad *and* stupid. 'You – have – to – be – invi—'

'I have,' Fred interrupted.

The twins gasped and their parents raised their eyebrows as Fred pulled the crumpled invitation from his pocket.

Wilbert snatched it.

'There's clearly been an administrative error,' he announced. 'This must be meant for us. *We're* the brilliant wizards.'

'Then why is there only *one* invitation?' Willow pointed out.

Wolf rolled his eyes. '*Obviously* they know we come as a pair. Like all great double acts. Vanish 'n' Trick … Boil 'n' Cauldron … Gobble 'n' Toads …'

'And Marvin and Fred!' laughed Wilda, Fred's youngest sister. She peered over Wilbert's shoulder. 'It's not a mistake. The invitation's addressed to Fred – it's even got the correct bedroom. *His.*'

The twins fell silent – but only for a moment.

'I've heard M.A.G.I.C. Camp's rubbish

anyway,' Wolf said. 'The professors don't know anything. The teachers at school are better.'

'Yeah,' Wilbert said. 'Most people get lost trying to find it anyway. I doubt M.A.G.I.C. Camp even exists.'

Then the twins left to sulk elsewhere.

'That's a real achievement, darling.' Fred's mum smiled. 'We're very proud of you. What an opportunity!'

'Thanks,' said Fred, before explaining his dilemma. So far, the family conversation had done little to make up his mind.

'Go,' said Wallace, Fred's eldest, most talented brother. 'I once had the chance, and didn't. I've wondered *what if?* ever since.'

'But – why didn't you go?' Fred asked.

Wallace grimaced and rotated his hand, as if checking his joints still worked properly.

'Wand-Whoosher's Wrist – a common injury for busy wizards. Mine flared up really badly. They'd have probably fixed it there if I'd gone. But I didn't even try, which I regret. I figured I'd get invited the next year, but it turns out if you decline an invitation, you don't get invited again.'

'Oh,' said Fred.

Fred thought about everything carefully. Perhaps camp was a chance to learn the more advanced magic that Merlin hadn't yet taught him. And a chance to prove that he *could* hold his own and cope with pressure. Perhaps he *would* regret not going ... And if Marvin ended up at M.A.G.I.C. School, and Fred didn't, would they drift apart? Fred hated that thought.

'Best get packing, Fred.' Wallace smiled, as if reading Fred's mind. 'It's only for three nights, and you'll have Marvin there. How bad could it be?'

Chapter Four

The next day, Fred stood outside the front door of his house, a bag slung over his shoulder. He studied the photo in his hands once more. Its image of M.A.G.I.C. Camp's buildings and grounds was seared on his mind after the hours he'd spent staring at it the previous evening.

It wasn't difficult to imagine the place; soft streaks of early-afternoon sunlight were casting patterns on the lawn in front of where Fred stood, and the photo showed a similarly serene autumnal scene. But inside Fred was feeling anything but serene. His overactive imagination often caused his worries to spiral out of control and helped him picture the worst-case scenario in all-too-vivid detail. He couldn't afford for that to happen now. Clicking himself to a place he'd never been would require every little bit of his focus.

Fred tucked the photo into his pocket and closed his eyes. Crisp air filled his nostrils and lungs as he took several deep, deliberate breaths. He tried to concentrate his mind on his destination, and urged his senses to feel what it might be like to be there: the

Wizards
Welcome!

cushion of the lush lawn beneath his feet; a breeze skimming his face as it rolled off the hills behind the woodland that encircled the grounds; the buzz made by eager wizards and witches chatting. Fred moved his thumb closer to the tip of his middle finger.

In the millisecond it took to snap them together, a doubt entered Fred's mind: *What if I can't do it?*

That was all it took to throw him off course.

Before he'd even opened his eyes, Fred knew he'd made a mistake. The atmosphere felt dense and heavy; the air he breathed was hot, and Fred realized he was far from home, and camp. The sun beat down from high in the sky, and the rough ground beneath his feet was baked solid as rock.

Something squawked near his head, and Fred forced his eyes open. Squinting in the glare of the sun, he saw little of the bird that had flown past.

As his eyes gradually adjusted, he spotted a large object in the distance that seemed to be moving slowly but purposefully towards him. Fred strained his neck forward and widened his eyes, trying to make it out.

A dusty jumble of brown and yellow and gold slinked and prowled closer.

How strange, Fred thought. *That looks an awful lot like a lion.*

It made no sense. He hadn't imagined *this* as he'd clicked his fingers. Surely it couldn't be a lion …

Fred was right.

It wasn't a lion.

It was two!

As they bounded towards him, Fred's stomach rolled over. What could he do?

Get out his wand?

That wouldn't frighten them, and he was yet to learn a lion-vanishing spell.

Run?

He was nippy, but not *lion*-fast.

Scream?

Cry?

Sing a song?

He had no time to choose, and the lions were almost upon him, roaring with hunger …

Click his fingers?

That was it!

Just as the lions leaped at him, teeth and claws exposed, Fred **SNAPPED** his fingers and vanished from sight.

Chapter Five

'You idiot!' Fred shouted, his heart hammering against his chest as he tried to work out where he was now.

He'd been reluctant to click himself home and start again, which probably would have been the sensible option, because failing to focus clearly and deliberately on a specific destination almost always led to a random outcome.

Directly in his eyeline was a stupendous, oversized pair of *very* bright and *very* shiny red shoes dotted with luminous yellow stars.

'*What* did you call me?'

Fred looked up. Staring down at him was an explosion of colour – a man dressed in a stripy rainbow wig and bow tie, with flamboyant chequered trousers held up by green braces that stretched over his spotted shirt. A huge red nose shone from the middle of a face caked in make-up. Everything about the clown's appearance was designed to look happy, but the only convincing thing about him was the dejection in his eyes.

'I'm not an idiot,' he said. 'This is just my job.'

Taking in the colour, laughter and honking

of horns all around, Fred realized he had somehow clicked himself into the middle of what appeared to be an enormous clown convention. He opened his mouth to apologize, but the clown was just getting started.

'I'm sick of people calling me names, laughing at me, thinking all I'm good for is clowning around!'

Isn't that kind of the point? Fred wanted to say, though he didn't.

'I'm worth more than *this*. I've got a PhD! And *feeling*s.'

'I'm sorry,' Fred said. 'I didn't mean—'

'No – it's *quite* all right,' the clown interrupted. 'Really, the joke's on you ...'

He raised his arm to his shoulder, and lined up his target.

As much as Fred liked pie, he didn't fancy
one in the face. He clicked his fingers once
more and departed.

This time Fred found himself not in immediate danger of death or humiliation by pie, but back outside his own house.

What was going wrong? It wasn't the actual clicking, for he'd managed to travel *somewhere* each time he'd tried. He'd done that bit – the physical *travelling* – so often it had become second nature. No, it was his lack of belief that was the problem. He needed to convince himself that he could click himself to camp, that he deserved to be there.

Fred took out the photo. He stared at it until he could practically see himself in the picture, standing in front of the magnificent higgledy-piggledy building that leaned wonkily in the middle of the beautiful grounds.

I can *do this. I'm* meant *to do this. I* will *do this.*

He repeated the words over and over again, until he uttered them without consciously trying.

Finally, with a solid, satisfying snap, he clicked his fingers.

Fred heard the laughter before he opened his eyes. It was uncontrollable and heartfelt, young and excited, not empty or forced like the clowns'.

He opened his eyes and was filled with relief. His view was an almost mirror image of the photo he was holding. He'd passed the first test. He'd made it to M.A.G.I.C. Camp.

As Fred looked around, he realized he was in the middle of a stage, and suddenly he understood that the laughter was directed at him. He'd clearly been holding up whatever performance the expectant crowd was

waiting for. Feeling exposed, Fred searched for his best friend's face in the audience.

Marvin's was one of the few faces not creased up with laughter. Marvin tilted his head in the direction of the empty seat next to him, and Fred hurriedly made his way to take his place next to his friend. The boy on Marvin's other side was still

giggling, and gave Fred a nasty look that he didn't appreciate.

'Glad you made it.' Marvin smiled, somewhat awkwardly. Was Fred imagining the embarrassed expression on Marvin's face?

As uncertainty swirled uncomfortably around Fred's mind, the murmuring crowd fell silent.

The opening ceremony was about to begin.

Chapter Six

Fireworks exploded high in the air, their sparkles and colours morphing into the shapes of people and animals that performed magical stories in the darkening evening sky.

Fred gasped with wonder as the witches and wizards onstage created incredible illusions that made the impossible seem real. Clouds parted and the stars came so close to the crowd that Fred could almost reach out and touch them. Lightning and thunder, walls of water and fire, were conjured and manipulated like puppets on a string.

One by one, the magicians transformed themselves into various objects – candlesticks, gingerbread men, plant pots, wheelbarrows – and back again, before taking on each other's identities, leaving their audience amazed and confused as to who was really who.

Fred was astonished when a vial containing a silver potion magically appeared in his hand. He looked at Marvin. He had one too. So did all the other audience members. Suddenly Fred felt an overwhelming urge to drink it, and, when he did, he experienced a wave of boundless joy, as if he would never again worry.

As Fred's feelings returned to their normal state, an elegant witch glided onto the stage. Her presence encouraged expectant silence.

'It is my pleasure to warmly welcome all of you to M.A.G.I.C. Camp! I trust that you enjoyed the show?' she said. 'My name is Professor Sue Perdoopa and I am Mistress of Magic here.

'Each of you with us tonight is a magician of astounding genius, intrepidness and courage. You were invited precisely because of those qualities. Every invitee has the magical potential to warrant their invitation, but not all are able to harness their skills and control their focus when it really counts. If you are here, you have passed the first test and you deserve your place at M.A.G.I.C. Camp. If you have doubts, and wish to leave at any point, please speak to a professor: due to the enchantment that's now in place, it is no longer possible for students to click-and-go around, in or out of the grounds.

'We aim to nurture your talent, to prepare you for your future as important magicians or leaders within the magical community. Yet I must remind you that with the gifts you have been given comes a responsibility to make the right choices. Respect your power. Use it wisely. Above all, be kind and be honest.

'The challenges you'll face over the next three days are designed to be fun, and to bring out the best in you. The closing ceremony, which you'll perform on Friday – independently or as a group, that's up to you – will be your opportunity to demonstrate what you have learned and persuade us that you deserve the prestigious M.A.G.I.C. Medal and a place at M.A.G.I.C. School –

which, as I'm sure you know, can set you apart as the best of the best. We look forward to it with immense excitement.

'And now, to bed!'

As everyone else groaned at the prospect of an early night, Fred, despite his fresh excitement at what the following days might bring, was grateful that a much-needed rest beckoned.

'What happens now?' Marvin asked.

As if prompted by the question, a group of goblins, sharp-nosed and pointy-eared, suddenly appeared from thin air. Fred struggled not to yelp at the sight of one goblin's rotten teeth that jutted from its mouth at impossible angles, adding menace to a face that seemed as if it had only ever looked surly. Its colleague hobbled around as if its left leg was six inches shorter than its right.

In spite of appearances, the goblins were charming. They declared themselves at everyone's service, and began leading individual wizards and witches across the lawn and into the main building towards their rooms.

'Let me sort that for you, sir,' one said to Fred as he moved to put his bag on his back. The goblin clapped his knobbly, long-fingered hands and Fred's bag disappeared from sight. Marvin laughed, until the goblin assigned to him vanished his bag too.

'Where have they gone?' Fred asked, alarmed.

'To your rooms, sir, where you will find their contents unpacked and arranged upon your arrival shortly. Shall we?'

The two goblins led them through narrow corridors and up winding staircases until they arrived at Marvin's room. Loitering in the neighbouring doorway was the wizard who'd sat next to Marvin during the opening ceremony.

'Hex,' he said, shaking Marvin's hand. 'Didn't properly introduce myself earlier. You seem familiar, somehow.'

'I'm Marvin – and this is Fred.'

'I knew it! I saw your photo in the newspaper.'

'It's nice to meet you, Hex.' Fred smiled. His outstretched hand was met with a sneer.

After what felt like an eternity, Hex silently shook it.

'Your room's on the next floor, sir,' the goblin informed Fred, interrupting the awkwardness, before setting off.

A little disappointed, Fred bid Marvin goodnight, then followed the goblin along the corridor and out of sight.

Chapter Seven

'GET UP! GET UP! GET UP!'

Fred was flung from the warm cocoon of his duvet onto the cold floor, and the shouting began again. To Fred's astonishment, it was coming from his bed – *belonged* to his bed: a bed with a life of its own.

'I SAID, GET UP! HONESTLY, BOY. GET A MOVE ON!'

Despite his sleepy confusion, Fred apologized, and, thinking it wise to keep his bed happy, started to make it.

'THERE'S NO TIME!' it wailed, before making itself. 'GET DRESSED OR YOU'LL MISS YOUR FIRST LESSON!'

Fred frantically put on the clothes that had materialized, neatly laid out on the bed.

'You've missed breakfast.' Right on cue, Fred's stomach rumbled. 'Eat this on your way.'

A slab of toast, slathered with peanut butter and banana, appeared on the bedside table. Fred took a grateful bite as he went to leave his room.

'WAIT! YOU DON'T EVEN KNOW WHERE YOU'RE GOING!'

That's true, Fred realized, and listened carefully to the instructions.

'Your first lesson is Tremendous Transformation. Go down the stairs, turn left, then open the door. It's through the arch, under the bridge, over the wall. Follow

the signs for the pigs. At the aardvark, make a U-turn and consider your life choices.'

'Excuse me?'

'Only joking,' the bed sighed. 'Everything you need – your timetable, directions – is in the booklet on the table over there. I'd have pointed it out last night, but you seemed too tired to take in anything. Anyway, let's speed things up: go to the end of the corridor, down the stairs, take two lefts and it's the first room on your right.'

'Thanks!' Fred grabbed the booklet and set off, wondering just what the day had in store.

Fred arrived to find Marvin sitting next to Hex. They were chatting like old friends. It was strange, Fred thought. He'd never actually seen Marvin with a friend other than him. At school, Marvin was usually on his own if he wasn't with Fred: his classmates tended to find his magic intimidating so they generally left him alone.

Fred took the unoccupied seat on Marvin's other side. Marvin nodded hello, but Hex barely looked up, and Fred's stomach did a little somersault as he heard Marvin laughing at something his new friend had said. Camp wasn't going to be just about him and Marvin, another double-act adventure. Fred wasn't sure how he felt about that.

He looked around the beautifully lit

classroom. He'd never seen so many weird curiosities: some looked as old as magic itself, while others could pass, Fred thought, as objects from the future. He recognized some of them: the tiny silver pot that he could see on the closest windowsill was actually a Cavernous Cauldron, which could store and conceal an infinite number of things, no matter their size. There was a Duplicity Detector too – a simple egg-shaped device that glowed orange when anyone within its vicinity was lying or misrepresenting the truth. But other objects, like the jar full of what looked a bit like floating golden butterflies, and the S-shaped stick with the claw of some unknown creature attached to its end, remained a mystery to him. He hoped he wouldn't be picked upon to explain them.

'Hey, Marv, what do you think—' Fred began when Marvin and Hex's conversation lulled, only to be interrupted.

'Remember that joke from last night? Hilarious!' Hex chuckled, and Marvin laughed too.

'What was the—' Fred tried to include himself, but the same thing happened.

'And that one you told me, about the unicorn, the troll and the toothbrush,' Hex interrupted. 'Disgusting!'

In fact, every time Fred opened his mouth to speak Hex interjected, deliberately, Fred noticed, to stop him joining in. He'd have assumed he was being paranoid, had it not been for the scathing looks Hex kept giving him over Marvin's shoulder. *What was his problem?*

Just then, the battered green filing cabinet at the front of the room began to wobble. It creaked loudly as it widened like an expanding balloon, before it **POPPED**. The class gasped, then applauded, as a gangly, older-than-middle-aged wizard stood, smiling, where the cabinet had been.

'Welcome, dear students. I am Professor Changer, and this is Tremendous Transformation – which, in my opinion, is the greatest of magical disciplines. Transformation is elegant and beautiful.' He pointed his wand at the walls of the classroom, which changed to depict a stunning skyline, so that Fred felt as if he was perched on a rooftop among chimneys, towers and spires, high above and gazing out across an enchanting, unknown city.

'It's quick and efficient, silent and stealthy.' Without appearing to do anything at all, Professor Changer plunged the classroom into darkness.

'And it's your friend when in danger.' Light returned to the classroom, which suddenly filled with the sound of screams as jagged rocks hurtled from nowhere towards the students, before being turned to balls of cotton wool with a flick of the professor's wand. One landed gently on Fred's shoulder.

'The skills of transformation can aid you in any situation and, if mastered, help you to overcome whatever problem you may face. Even a basic grasp of the more advanced elements will get you far.'

'So,' Professor Changer continued, 'your

goal today is to use transformation techniques to make yourself unrecognizable.'

A collective murmur of excitement followed. Fred watched his classmates size each other up, and he could feel the competitiveness escalating around him. He noticed Marvin sit a little taller in his seat, and Hex smirk and puff out his chest, totally self-assured. Fred didn't hope to be the best – just to keep up – but when he met eyes with Hex, the disdainful look he received did nothing to boost his confidence.

'First, we must warm up our minds and our magic, so let's practise some basic transformations.'

Fred studied the items that had appeared on his desk: a toadstool, a toilet roll, a pie and a pin. He listened to Professor Changer's reminders about the importance of proper posture, wand movement, visualization and commitment. He willed the toadstool to become a toad, then waved his wand as precisely as he could …

The transformation wasn't *perfect*; the toad was red and spotty, much like the toadstool had been. But it *was* a toad, and pretty good for a first attempt, especially given the distracting sniggers that Fred knew had been coming from Hex. Why couldn't Hex concentrate on his own transformations? Doing his best to ignore the sniggers, he waved his wand again, completing the toad's transformation, before glancing sideways to check on his classmates' progress.

One witch was clearly having a few difficulties: her wand's behaviour was as eccentric as her appearance. It kept shooting jets of water at random, QUACKED! and OINKED! whenever she tried a spell, and occasionally flew out of her hand across the room. Fred saw as she went to retrieve it that she was wearing odd shoes and a hat that was drowning in badges making statements such as 'Serpents aren't servants!', 'Wizards 4 Lizards', and 'I ♥ Toads'. But apart from her, everyone appeared on track.

Some students had already changed two of their items, but Fred felt relieved that he was more or less keeping up with the pace. Unsurprisingly, Marvin had no problems, and neither did Hex. Their toads were bathing happily in the toilets that they'd produced from the toilet rolls, while two little magpies poked their beaks out of the pockets of the pinafores in which the two boys were prancing around, amusing their classmates.

Fred had always admired Marvin's brilliance, but now he felt a sensation he

realized was envy. How was it fair that Marvin and Hex seemed to find magic so effortless, when for him it required so much focus? Judging by some of his classmates' expressions, they felt much the same.

Worse was the sight of Marvin having so much fun with someone other than Fred. He seemed delighted to have found a young

wizard as capable – perhaps even *better* – at magic than he was. It was just a shame that that someone seemed to sneer with disapproval whenever he looked at Fred.

Chapter Eight

When it was time for the next task, Fred was half a pie behind his classmates; as their birds fluttered their wings around him, he stared with frustration at the mix of pastry and feathers that represented his efforts.

He was confused. The connection between his mind and his wand seemed to be working well – so why wasn't his magic? It was as if an invisible force was interfering, somehow. Was it nerves? Although he tried to ignore them, Hex's sniggers were definitely affecting his concentration. Was Hex directly affecting his *magic* too? Maybe that was the reason …

Professor Changer clapped his hands. 'Now, working in pairs, I want you to practise changing your partner's appearance. Remember, transforming your own or another human's appearance is trickier than working with lifeless objects or small creatures. It's risky. Mistakes are difficult to correct.'

Fred and Marvin exchanged an amused glance, remembering the time Marvin had given them super-sized ears to improve their hearing, without knowing the counter-spell to change them back. Some of Fred's jealously drained away. Professor Changer advised everyone to start with something small and risk-free, like changing the colour of their partner's clothing, before building up to trickier transformations.

'Right. Pair up and begin!'

Fred turned to Marvin, but Hex beat him to it.

'Want to start, or shall I?'

Marvin squirmed, looking between Hex and Fred. Fred smiled awkwardly. Hex raised his eyebrows.

'Actually, Hex, I was going to work with Fred,' Marvin grimaced. 'Sorry.'

Hex scoffed. 'But we're much better matched.'

'We could probably work as a three?' Fred suggested, as a way to prevent Marvin from having to choose between them. He'd glanced around the classroom and, although some students were still moving about and swapping places to partner up, it appeared that most pairs had already been formed. As well as wanting to work with Marvin, who he'd barely had a chance to talk to, he wanted to show Hex that he wasn't a pushover.

'You're going to keep up with *us*?' Hex snorted.

Fred attempted not to sound hurt.

'I can try. Marvin normally helps me. He's a great teacher.'

'Fine,' Hex sighed. 'Just don't embarrass me.'

But before Fred had the chance, Professor Changer addressed the class. He was standing next to the eccentric-looking girl, who was on her own. Fred could see why the other students had avoided her. As well as her misfiring wand, odd shoes and statement badges, she had pink, wavy hair and wore gold-framed, star-shaped glasses that exaggerated her slightly dreamy expression. Fred thought she looked as if she had arrived at M.A.G.I.C. Camp by mistake. Perhaps that explained her troubles with her wand, too – maybe she just wasn't very good.

'Is anybody else without a partner?'

When nobody raised their hands, Hex took matters into his own.

'Fred is.'

'Perfect. Join Grace over here, Fred.'

Hex smirked and wished Fred luck, a bit sarcastically, Fred thought. Marvin didn't say anything.

Still, Grace's smile and the kindness in

her eyes were better than Hex's sneers.

'Good evening,' she said, when Fred sat down.

He checked the time – mainly to see which one of them was mad. It was eleven-fifteen. In the morning.

'Just testing.' Grace winked. 'You passed!'

'Great,' Fred smiled, confused.

'Shall we get started?' Grace raised her wand, which Fred now saw was kinked at the end.

'Isn't that *broken*?' he said, fearing for his safety. He'd noticed earlier how unpredictable it was.

Grace smiled. 'Out of sorts, perhaps. Some of the girls borrowed – well, *stole* – it last night. I *did* think it looked odd when I found it. It's been a bit erratic – but I think I'm getting the hang of it now. What colour shall we make your cloak? Ooh, red will suit you!'

'Sure,' Fred muttered, glancing over to where Hex was high-fiving Marvin, who had transformed Hex's outfit so that it acted as a mirror. Fred noticed his downturned expression. He tried to look cheerful and ignore the ache between his stomach and throat.

'Red for Fred,' Grace chuckled. She placed her wand, the bent tip of which pointed upwards, on Fred's cloak, then tapped it three times.

'Ouch!' Fred was more shocked than injured, but still a bit alarmed by the sight of his new bulbous, shiny red nose reflected in Hex's outfit. Professor Changer, unaware the result was an accident, led a smattering of applause, which Fred noticed seemed to irk Hex. Fred's cloak, meanwhile, remained blue.

'See?' Grace grimaced. 'It *sort of* works. It's just hard to direct. Sorry.'

Fred accepted her apology, but they spent the next fifteen minutes trying to fix his nose, which was now throbbing painfully. After Professor Changer had stepped in, and also, after some complicated magic, fixed Grace's wand, he explained the final challenge.

'You'll each have two minutes to transform yourself. During that time, the rest of the class will be blindfolded, like this –' he flicked his wand and everyone's vision blurred until he lifted the spell – 'and then we'll try to spot how you're disguised.'

Fred tried to think how he could disguise himself. He thought he'd be unable to do something as complicated as conceal his identity when his nerves were starting to get the better of him again. He'd just have to try, and hope.

Still, not all of Fred's classmates found the task easy. Some were spotted within seconds, having made unsuccessful attempts to change their legs to stacks of books, or their arms to umbrellas. There were some brilliant transformations too. Marvin camouflaged himself to blend in perfectly with the map of the world that stretched from the floor to the ceiling, and, standing in front of it, proved difficult to spot. Grace disguised herself as an old armchair in the back corner of the room, which Fred thought was brilliant. But one stripy sock remained on show, which was the thing that gave her away.

Hex's disguise bettered everyone's. He was perfectly concealed amongst the furniture, having transformed himself to resemble a grandfather clock. After he'd BONGED loudly, enjoyed his classmates' applause, and returned to his seat, it was Fred's turn.

Fred looked around for inspiration. He attempted to blend in with the wooden door of the classroom, but couldn't get the grain-effect right. He gave himself a top hat and a moustache, which only made his top lip itch. With time running out and slight panic clouding his thoughts, Fred conjured

something to hide behind: why it turned out
to be a garish windbreak remained a mystery
to him. If anything, it drew *more* attention
to him, especially as his hat remained visible
even once he'd crouched behind it.

'So, can anyone spot Fred?' he heard Professor Changer ask.

There were a few poorly stifled giggles before Fred heard Hex's scornful voice.

'More like can anyone *not* spot Fred.'

Thankfully the bell rang to drown out the sound of further giggles and signal the end of the lesson. The lump in Fred's throat took a moment to disappear.

As everyone filed out of the room, Fred looked for Marvin. He hoped to have a proper chance to chat, for a bit of reassurance. But Marvin had already left.

Wanting to find him, Fred dashed past Grace, barely acknowledging her invitation to have lunch together.

Chapter Nine

Fred weaved along the corridor through the crowd of hungry, chattering students, searching for Marvin.

When he reached the high-ceilinged dining hall, teetering towers of food obscured the faces of the ravenous witches and wizards sitting at the long, broad tables.

'Fred, over here!'

Marvin, for the first time since they'd

arrived at camp, appeared to be by himself.

'Sorry, I meant to wait for you but got pulled along by the crowd rushing for lunch. I'd heard rumours it was good, but this is *amazing*!'

Fred nodded, looking at the delicious banquet in front of them.

'Didn't I tell you camp would be brilliant?' Marvin said. 'I did more magic in that one lesson than in the last year at school. I'm actually learning something for once.'

'Mmm-hmm,' Fred mumbled through a mouthful of food, taken aback. He was pleased Marvin was enjoying camp, especially when he'd wanted to come for so long, so the last thing Fred wanted to do was bring Marvin down by revealing that he *wasn't* having a particularly good time. Though surely Marvin could already see that? Hadn't he noticed Fred's embarrassment at the end of the lesson, and Hex's rudeness? It appeared not. Perhaps, Fred thought, Marvin was just overexcited.

'And not just from the teachers,' Marvin continued. 'I think Hex is even better at magic than I am! You should have seen the spells he was doing last night!'

'Where is he now?' Fred asked. He wondered if the only reason Marvin was talking normally to him now was because Hex wasn't here.

'He went to the toilet. Why?'

Fred pushed his food around his plate. 'Just wondered.'

Marvin couldn't miss the coolness in Fred's voice.

'Are you all right?' he asked.

Not really, but why can't you see it? Why didn't you wait for me, honestly? Why didn't you stand up for me? Fred thought, but didn't say. He felt he was losing his friend to someone else, but tried to reassure himself that things would return to normal soon. Camp was short. He could cope.

'It's just …' Fred tried to keep his voice level. 'That wasn't the *greatest* lesson for me …'

'I'm sorry we couldn't work together,' Marvin began. 'I did try to—'

'It's not just that.' Emotion bubbled inside Fred. 'I think I'm losing my magic again. Even when I was doing everything right, *something* stopped it working. And at the end of that lesson, I felt really stupid – embarrassed.'

'Embarrassed? By *me*?'

'No – by Hex! Don't you think his comments were a bit mean, Marv? He's been giving me nasty looks ever since I arrived.'

'Fred, you're overreacting. I suppose he can be a little impatient, but maybe he doesn't understand that some people find magic more difficult than he does. He's not *nasty*,' Marvin tried to reassure him.

'Well, he's not exactly been friendly either. He doesn't seem to like me very much.'

Marvin frowned. 'What reason would Hex have not to like you?'

'I don't know. You tell me – you seem to know everything about him,' Fred said, instantly regretting it when he saw a flash of anger in Marvin's eyes.

'Now you just sound jealous.'

The silence that followed said everything. The boys looked at each other, aware that their friendship had entered unknown territory.

'I'm sorry, Marv. Maybe I am jealous. I just thought you'd realize how I was feeling and stick up for me. That we'd stick together, like we always do.'

Marvin's expression softened, but his reply thumped Fred in the chest.

'But what about how *I'm* feeling? I can't always be thinking about how you're getting on, wondering whether you need my help. Sometimes I have to do what *I* need. I'm pleased you made it here, you *deserve* to be here, but you can cope without me. Maybe it's good that we don't do *everything* together.' With that, Marvin got up from the table and disappeared into the crowd.

Too late Fred realized he'd done the opposite of what he'd hoped: he'd pushed Marvin away.

Hex appeared, looking for Marvin. When all he found was Fred, he made his disappointment clear.

'Why are you even here?'

'Lunch,' Fred mumbled.

'*No* – at camp, generally. You don't belong. You're not here because you're good at magic, only because you're famous. It's ridiculous. *You're* ridiculous.'

Fred didn't have the will to argue. He was still thinking about his conversation with Marvin. Was Marvin right? Did Fred rely on him too much? 'I think Marvin's looking for you. He just left,' he said quietly.

Hex looked towards where Fred was pointing, and turned to go. 'Maybe you should leave too.'

For probably the only time ever, Fred thought, *I agree with you.*

Chapter Ten

Fred only half-heard the words of his professor as he sat in the Potions classroom at the top of the tallest tower in the grounds and stared blankly out at the slate-grey sky. It perfectly matched his mood. Every so often, he turned to glance at Marvin to catch a sense of how he was feeling. Was he still cross? Was he sorry for what he said? Marvin's expression gave little away.

'There are concoctions to make you invisible, that allow you to fly, see into the future and look into the past. Potions can enrich or erode life, extend or extinguish it. But mastery of Potions requires a talent and determination that only the very best wizards or witches possess. And you are the very best of the future.'

Professor Draught proceeded to demonstrate important practical elements of advanced potion-making: how to handle and measure ingredients; effective stirring techniques; how to bottle and store the finished product, among other things. The steady rhythm of pops and snaps, fizzing and bubbling, helped capture Fred's attention whenever his thoughts drifted towards the tear in his friendship with Marvin, towards Hex's comments, towards home. He was sorely tempted to leave camp, to take the easy option, but the more he considered it, the less sense it seemed to make. Giving up wouldn't help. It would only prove Hex right, and Fred was determined to prove him *wrong*. He wanted – no, *needed* – the medal. He was sure Marvin would earn one and go on to M.A.G.I.C. School, which meant he had to earn his as well – their friendship depended on it. He couldn't bear the thought of them drifting even further apart. Staying was his only option.

Challenged to brew a potion to transform, delight or entertain Professor Draught by the end of the lesson, Fred dragged himself to join the queue of students poring over the ingredients on offer. Three towering columns of tall, thin wooden shelves dominated the biggest wall of the room. Signs at the top of each one explained how they were organized by category: **Ingredients: Creatures, Ingredients: Plants, Ingredients: Herbs**. To Fred's relief, every vial, jar, pot, box and flask arranged along the shelves was carefully labelled in the same immaculate script that outlined their contents and how and why they might be used. **Dragon Dust** jostled for space with **Troll Tears** and **Hag's Hair**, whilst **Jinxroot**, **Squizzleworm Seeds** and **Hemplepumple** nestled next to each other. Those were merely the ingredients Fred could see from the back of the line.

He wondered how such exotic, mysterious ingredients were sourced. It was surely a treacherous venture, requiring courage – which got Fred thinking …

By the time Fred was opposite the shelves, the selection was sparser than before, but he grabbed a few jars containing ingredients he thought might suit his plans and returned to his workstation.

Professor Draught watched over proceedings, grinning at the students' careful efforts. The hush of concentration was punctuated only by the occasional clang of a hard ingredient dropping onto a metal weighing scale, or the soft frothing and high-pitched popping of bubbles as students added to or stirred their potions.

Fred could see a silky, silver mist rising from Marvin's cauldron, emitting a sweet, friendly, relaxing aroma. Hex's potion spat steadily from its container, but he looked content, as if all was going to plan.

Fred examined the labels on each of the ingredients he'd selected; **Horned Frog Heart**, for perseverance, an **Eagle Eye**, for spotting danger and opportunity, and **Brickseed**, for strength of character and body. He sliced the heart into tiny, equal pieces as instructed, then dropped them one by one into his cauldron of boiling water precisely every seven seconds. As the liquid began to shimmer, he squeezed the shiny eye over the pot until it burst with a squawk before fizzling in the mix. After stirring until his elbow ached, he added the seed that he'd crumbled to a powder, which crackled and popped like corn kernels in a hot pan.

Fred realized he'd forgotten to add something of himself. As he chewed the nail off his finger, Hex passed him on his way towards the shelves of ingredients and, to Fred's surprise, mumbled, 'Marvin wants to talk to you.' *Maybe we're all right, after all*, Fred thought. He dropped his fingernail into his cauldron. His potion, turning gold, simmered nicely.

When Fred approached, Marvin barely looked up.

'I'm busy. What do you want, Fred?'

'Didn't you want to talk to me?'

Marvin looked at Fred with the same

confusion Fred was feeling, then over Fred's shoulder.

'You'd better get back to your potion.'

Fred, horrified, saw his potion spitting violently out of the cauldron. He sprinted back – brushing shoulders with Hex who was returning to his station – and lunged for a lid. He was too late. The potion erupted. Fred's concoction for courage pooled around his feet.

But I did everything right, Fred thought.

He looked around the room, searching for an explanation. He acknowledged Grace's sympathetic smile with a shrug. Some of his classmates glanced up briefly, before returning to their potions. Then Fred saw Hex's smirk – and everything made sense.

'You sabotaged my potion.' Fred tried to control his anger.

Marvin jumped to Hex's defence. 'Don't be ridiculous, Fred.'

'I'm not! It was going perfectly until *he* did something to it behind my back.' Fred pointed at Hex. '*That's* why you said Marvin wanted to talk to me.'

Hex looked back and forth between Fred and Fred's outstretched finger, but

Fred didn't get the hint.

'Or could it simply be that frog's heart and human blood are not a good mix?' Hex smugly suggested. 'Your finger,' he added.

Fred finally understood Hex's gesture. Blood was trickling from where he'd bitten the edge of his finger too hard. *Had* he accidentally added a drop to his potion with his fingernail? He wasn't certain Hex was telling the truth, but he couldn't prove he was lying either. He returned, embarrassed, to his workstation.

As Professor Draught began to sample everyone's potions, Hex oozed confidence. His only real competition was Marvin, whose potion instantly made the professor smile.

'A very impressive memory potion –

exceptionally difficult to brew! Congratulations, Marvin.'

Next up was Hex. As soon as his potion touched Professor Draught's lips, he broke into fits of giggles, and everyone *else* laughed. But the giggling turned to hiccups, then to snorts, and finally, uncontrollable sneezing. He looked thoroughly uncomfortable. A few students looked concerned. Like Fred, they thought Hex's potion verged on being unkind.

Professor Draught eventually stopped sneezing and, to his credit, brushed off his embarrassment, admitting that for sheer strength and effectiveness, Hex's potion deserved to be crowned the winner.

'*Unless*,' he continued, 'our last candidate

can do something extraordinary.'

He turned to Fred, who, to everyone's surprise, given his earlier disaster, handed him a potion. He held it up to the light. It was a rich, red colour, thick like gravy. He pulled out the stopper, dipped the tip of his little finger into the mixture, and placed it on his tongue.

'How … *interesting.*'

Fred's classmates leaned forward in their seats, eager to know what he'd brewed.

'Well, I asked that your potions entertain, transform or delight me, and *this –*' the professor said, before downing the remaining liquid – 'is *THE* most *DELGHTFUL*, *DELICIOUS* potion I have EVER tasted!'

The class gasped. Hex, visibly angry,

did not join in with the spontaneous ripple of applause. He whispered something to Marvin, who nodded and shot Fred a look – one he found hard to decipher, but didn't like.

'Fred, what on earth is it?' Professor Draught asked. 'It reminds me of … *tomato soup.*'

'Well, that's, err … *exactly* what it is. It's all I had time to make after my courage potion went wrong.'

'*Bravo!*' Professor Draught chuckled. 'A wonderfully balanced tomato soup – the best potion of the day!'

After that, Fred left the lesson smiling.

Hex, meanwhile, did not.

Chapter Eleven

'Honestly, how do you do it, Fred?'

Fred hadn't expected to find Marvin waiting for him in the corridor outside the classroom. He was even more surprised when Hex walked away to give them space, though the sinister smile he received from Hex as he departed was all too predictable. It appeared that Marvin now *did* want to talk. His tone was cold; he clearly didn't want to share in Fred's triumph about what had happened at the end of their Potions lesson.

'Do what?' Fred was baffled. 'Are you annoyed about the soup thing? I thought you'd find that funny. Anyway, it serves Hex right for wrecking my potion.'

Marvin barrelled on.

'You know – how do you win people over all the time? Steal the limelight. Always make *everything* about *you.*'

Resentment tinged his words. They stung Fred's ears and jabbed his heart.

'It must be luck,' Marvin said coldly, 'because it's not magic.'

Fred couldn't believe it. The person in front of his eyes suddenly seemed more like a stranger than his best friend. But it made saying what he wanted to say to Marvin much easier.

'Are these *your* words, or Hex's? Is that what you were discussing before I arrived? Because you're beginning to sound just like him.'

'Well, he's right! How *you* got invited here is a mystery even to me! And even now, when it's *my* time to shine, you *still* manage to make it all about you—'

'You should have just said if you didn't want me to come—' Fred tried to interrupt. But Marvin wasn't finished.

'I'm fed up – of always being the overshadowed sidekick of Famous Fred, never getting any credit. Is the glory, the praise, the special friendship with Merlin not enough, Fred? What more do you want? Can't you cope with me having a friendship that isn't with you?'

In spite of the hurtful words cascading from Marvin's mouth, Fred stood his ground, wiping his tears away with his sleeve, aware of the crowd of students who had gathered in the corridor.

'What I can't understand is why you *like* him,' Fred replied. 'And don't pretend that he hasn't been nasty – he said to my face that he thinks I don't deserve to be here, and he ruined my potion, I know it!'

'He didn't!' Marvin protested. 'You're jealous, Fred. You made a mess of your potion – *exactly* like all the other times

you've made a mess of something magical! And Hex is right: you *have* held me back. I've had enough of it.'

Fred felt as if he'd been punched in the stomach. All he wanted was to disappear. But his body felt heavy; his feet stuck to the ground. He barely mustered the energy to raise his gaze to Marvin.

When he did, he was surprised to see that Marvin too was rubbing tears from his cheeks. He'd sensed Marvin was angry, but not *sad* – he'd never seen him so upset, nor realized his feelings were so strong.

The crowd, sensing the drama was over, began to disperse, a faint purr of chatter filling the corridor as witches and wizards made their way to dinner or whatever evening activity awaited them.

When Fred looked up again, Marvin had gone.

Chapter Twelve

Fred remained in the corridor. He was barely aware of how much time had passed since he'd slumped onto the floor after his argument with Marvin. He guessed he'd probably missed dinner, not that he'd have wanted to go anyway. He let the wall support the weight of his muddled head. It was pounding, as if the thoughts knocking into one another inside it were physical objects, hammering at his skull.

What happened? In less than twenty-four hours, he and Marvin had gone from being best friends to bitter ... not quite *enemies* ... but what felt like strangers; from being inseparable to hardly able to meet one another's eyes. The reservations he'd had about attending camp suddenly seemed justified, though he hadn't, of course, imagined he'd fall out so spectacularly with Marvin.

More importantly, *how* had it happened – and so *fast?* Perhaps he should have thought more carefully about what Marvin wanted and left him to enjoy camp on his own; after all, Marvin's reaction to his invitation hadn't exactly been enthusiastic. But Marvin had never explicitly said, 'Don't come.' And anyway, it felt bigger than that now, as if a dark force, some menacing magic, had tormented then swallowed their friendship. As far as Fred was concerned, there'd been no major problem until Hex had come between them, but now it was as though Marvin was under Hex's spell …

A fresh thought disturbed Fred: perhaps *Hex* was the dark force. Was Hex using magic to come between them, to try to prove a point about Fred? He was certainly clever enough. And now, every time he thought about it, Fred felt more and more certain that Hex had sabotaged his potion, maybe even his magic in Transformation. So was Marvin *literally* under Hex's spell?

But then … *was* he always stealing the attention away from Marvin and everyone else? He never intended to, so how could Marvin blame him for that?

And, until now, Marvin had never seemed to resent Fred's success. He'd always been there for him – always happy to listen to and discuss Fred's worries. It was Marvin who'd encouraged Fred to take on the lizard – which had led to his friendship with Merlin. Marvin had only ever seemed excited about that.

But Fred's stomach lurched as a truth suddenly hit him with the force of the fiercest spell: he *had* too often been caught up in the bubble of his own world to notice how Marvin was feeling, not quite as good a friend as Marvin had always been to him. He should have kept his worries about Hex to himself – dealt with them himself – rather than rely on Marvin for support, just as he always did. Camp was only for three days – why couldn't he have just kept quiet and held it together for Marvin?

Fred considered again whether he should just go home. That way, Marvin would be free to enjoy the rest of camp and focus on himself for once.

But then, why should he? Whatever Hex had said, Fred knew he deserved to be here, just as much as anyone else who'd passed the first task. Why shouldn't he be in with a chance to win a M.A.G.I.C. Medal? And if he went, wouldn't he be giving up on his and

Marvin's friendship? Surely the best option was to try to prove to Marvin how much it meant to him, to stick around and repair it? And, if he *was* right about Hex and things between Hex and Marvin turned sour, he needed to have his best friend's back.

No, tomorrow he'd find Marvin and apologize, promise to be a more selfless friend in the future – *if* there was any future friendship to be had. And he'd prove that awful Hex wrong too.

As he stumbled groggily down the corridor, he passed the board on which the evening activities on offer were displayed. Maybe a distraction was a better idea than spending the rest of the evening alone in his room.

He looked down the list for something that promised to be quiet, peaceful and, he hoped, not very popular. Broomstick Racing, Wand Wars, Speed Sorcery – not exactly what he had in mind.

But Magical Meditation?

That seemed ideal.

EVENING ACTIVITIES

Broomstick Racing

Wand Wars

Speed Sorcery

Magical Meditation

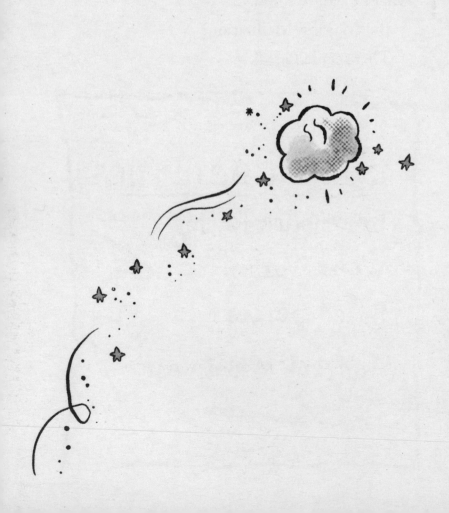

Chapter Thirteen

Fred pushed open the door and stepped into the room.

He screamed, then twisted backwards in a lurch for safety, hoping his fingertips would connect with the doorframe and prevent a long, terrifying plummet to his death. They didn't.

But Fred's foot found solid ground.

The blue sky that spread below his feet as

far as he could see was an illusion.

Once he'd regained his composure, Fred saw that he wasn't alone. The room was silent, save for the gentle blowing of a breeze, but there were two other people here. Each sat, eyes closed, on a perfect, puffy cloud. One was a man dressed in flowing white robes and a matching hat, which made it appear

as if he was growing out of the cloud itself. And opposite him, was Grace.

Fred tiptoed across the floor and collapsed onto a cloud, which felt even more comfortable than it looked. It massaged the tension and pain out of his body. He let out a long sigh. Slowly, his heavy eyes closed.

'Hello, Fred!'

'Oh. Hi,' Fred said, his eyes popping open again. Grace's eyes were still shut. 'How did you know it was me?'

'This is the sort of place I'd want to be after an argument like the one you just had.'

'So you saw that too,' Fred sighed.

'Most of it,' said Grace. 'Are you all right?'

Fred found himself nodding. As much as he wanted to talk, he was wary of doing what he always did – offloading his worries onto someone else. He tried to change the subject, and gestured towards the man in white. 'Who's he? Shouldn't we be quiet?'

'He's leading our session,' Grace explained.

'Are you *sure*?' Fred said. The man was so perfectly still and silent that he didn't seem to be doing *anything* – breathing included.

'Is he … *alive?*'

Grace finally opened her eyes.

'He's fine,' she said nonchalantly, before giving Fred a sympathetic smile. She seemed to sense that he wanted to talk, so took the initiative. 'If I were you, Fred, I'd give Marvin a little space, that's all. I bet he's feeling as confused as you. From what I overheard, you may have been a *bit* too focused on yourself at times, but I don't think you've been a bad friend.'

'You don't?'

'No. It's not your fault if the limelight always falls on you – you don't control that. Even if Marvin does deserve more credit, it doesn't mean you don't deserve yours. Weren't you alone when you came face to face with the lizard?'

'I was, but—'

'Didn't you work together to rescue Merlin from Kazam?'

'Well, yes, I cracked the clue that led us to them, but—'

'And aren't you *here* at M.A.G.I.C. Camp, having travelled and arrived all by yourself?'

'Obviously, but—'

'See?' Grace chuckled.

Fred smiled. Grace had the measure of him – like she'd known him for years, not hours. He felt guilty that he'd let her appearance cloud his initial judgement of her, that he'd been so preoccupied by his worries about Marvin's friendship with Hex that he hadn't thanked her for being so friendly as soon as they'd met. He realized that she wasn't lonely or strange, but introverted and wise, at ease with herself and her place in the world. And now, as she acted like the friend he needed, he realized Grace reminded him of Merlin: she too had an aura of kindness that made Fred feel at ease.

'And you don't think I'm mad to be suspicious of Hex?' he asked.

'Far from it,' Grace sighed. 'I think he's trouble. Hopefully Marvin will eventually see that too. As for Hex spoiling your potion, I didn't see *exactly* what he did – he had his back to me – but he lingered by your workstation. He was definitely up to no good. He's wrong about your "mistake" too.'

Fred raised his eyebrows. Hex had made

the claim with such authority that Fred assumed it was an indisputable fact. But, Fred thought, if Hex had tampered with his potion, it was equally likely he *had* been sabotaging his magic too!

'How can you be so sure?' he asked.

'I've picked up a few things from my parents – they're experts in magical creatures. Plus, they *constantly* talk about the creatures they've encountered – horned frogs, for instance – and their passion's infectious. Or maybe it's just in our blood – which, by the way, I can say with certainty would *not* react with the heart of a horned frog in the way Hex suggested.'

'That's amazing!' Fred said.

Grace smiled. 'They're away for work a

lot, which is tough – except when they take me with them! I've learned that magical monsters, like most rare, unfamiliar things, are often misunderstood. They're feared, but for the wrong reasons. Really, they need to be treated no differently to the way witches and wizards should treat each other. With respect and kindness. That's what my parents have taught me, anyway.'

'It shows.' Fred smiled. 'By the way, I thought what you did in Transformation was amazing – once your wand was fixed, I mean. Are the girls who stole it still causing you trouble?'

'No. I think now they've seen that I *do know* how to use it, they're scared I might transform them if they try anything. And so they should be.' Grace winked, making Fred laugh.

'Have you thought about your performance for the final ceremony?' she asked.

Fred shook his head. He'd figured he and Marvin would do something together. Now, even if they did make friends, he thought

Marvin would probably be teaming up with Hex. He didn't have a Plan B. *Unless …*

'Hey, want to work together for it?'

Grace's face lit up. 'Of course. Who better to pair up with than the tomato-soup brewing champion?'

'Exactly!' Fred bowed extravagantly and laughed. It felt good.

'Any ideas?' Grace asked.

'None.' Fred grimaced. 'Which is worrying with less than forty-eight hours to go.'

'Me neither. But at least we can be clueless together.'

Grace's words drove away the loneliness that Fred had felt since arriving at camp. He tried to find the words to express exactly what her kindness meant to him. Sometimes, the most complicated things require the simplest words.

'Thanks, Grace. Really. Thank you.'

Chapter Fourteen

The next morning, Fred, despite some nerves, shared the obvious excitement of his peers as he made his way to the first lesson of the day. Monster Management was considered too specialist and potentially dangerous a subject to be taught at normal schools, and was one of the things that made M.A.G.I.C. Camp so special. Rumours abounded about the creatures the students might encounter: unicorns, spiders, serpents, phoenixes or fire-breathing dragons. Timmy and Tammy, twins from a town called, coincidentally, Twinmouth, who, Fred had noticed, always looked tense and twitchy, seemed prepared for every eventuality, appearing in a variety of protective clothing and headgear. Other students were drowning in high-tech bits of equipment.

Despite the trepidation, Fred was disappointed to discover that the lesson, or at least the start of it, was to take place in a dusty old classroom. He scanned the room to see if Marvin was alone, but, as usual, he and Hex were deep in conversation. His apology would have to wait until later.

'Where are all the creatures?' Fred heard someone moan.

'Why aren't we outside?' wondered Wynona, a witch who had told Fred that at home she spent every waking moment outdoors.

The protests stopped abruptly when Professor Narly stomped into the room. Her smile, friendly though it was, did little to soften her harsh appearance. Fred gulped at the sight of her. The gaping C-shaped space where (Fred assumed) the rest of her thickset neck had once been was so alarming that it was almost possible to overlook the network of scars that ran like tributaries across her weathered face. Fred hoped her injuries were an ironic coincidence, rather than a sign of what her students should expect to look like by the end of the morning. Still, Professor Narly clearly spent her life around dangerous animals: the rough edges of her booming voice told of endless hours talking to the creatures in her care, which was, Fred deduced using the law of averages, bound to lead to at least a *few* unfortunate accidents. Nevertheless, Fred was entranced when she spoke.

'Think of this lesson as a taste of what it might be like to encounter, care for or work with magical animals. We can't cover all there is to know about them, but a little knowledge can serve you well,' she explained, before outlining the most important rules and principles of dealing with magical monsters. 'Disrespect and disobey them – and my instructions – at your peril.' Her cheerful grin was not reflected on the faces of her apprehensive students.

When she could see her students were too restless to focus on any more theory, Professor Narly led the group out of the classroom and into the grounds. Not far from the woodland, she stopped.

'What do you see?'

Fred couldn't see anything significant. Most of the other students shrugged their shoulders too.

Next to him, Grace, scanning the ground with her eyes, was the first to spot them. 'Tracks,' she said.

Professor Narly nodded. 'Look closely, everyone.'

Now that Grace had pointed them out, Fred easily spotted the prints of two large paws and what appeared to be the talons of a sizeable raptor. He had no idea what sort of creature they belonged to. It looked as if some sort of giant cat had tussled with a bird that could run but not fly away.

The trail was faint, but it was regular, and led into the woods ahead. The class followed it to a large clearing in the shadows of the gently swaying trees.

There, Fred's eyes rested on an enormous transparent box, in which several gigantic, limbless creatures squirmed. The group's collective groan of disappointment burst the bubble of excitement. Fred was confused. Surely these weren't the creatures that had made the tracks they had followed?

'*Really?*' Hex moaned. 'Worms?'

'Uh, uh, uh!' Professor Narly waggled her finger. 'What's the first rule of monster management?'

Grace's hand shot up. '*Respect the creature you have the privilege of meeting.*'

'Exactly.' Professor Narly waved her wand and a hole opened in the glasscase, out of which a worm slowly emerged. 'They may look ordinary – apart from their size, of course – but these are *rainbow* worms. Rare, marvellous creatures. Now, a volunteer ...'

She looked at Fred, who, desperately wanting not to be picked, kept his arms tightly by his sides.

'Perfect! Thank you, Fred.' Professor Narly grabbed Fred's cloak and dragged him towards the worm. Fred glanced at Marvin, as if to make clear that becoming the centre of attention often *wasn't* his choice. 'Our resident lizard expert should find this easy,' she chuckled. 'Now, follow my instructions. First, you must interact on *their* terms. So, Fred, down on your belly!'

She gave Fred an encouraging shove. His

mouth filled with dirt as he hit the ground.

'Oops. Are you all right? Excellent. Now, when it moves forward, do so too. When you're close enough, touch noses.'

Fred obediently followed Professor Narly's instructions, ignoring his classmates' sniggers and his embarrassment at being made to slither around like a worm. But when the professor told him to sing the lullaby intended to charm the worm into lighting up, his self-consciousness overpowered his desire not to fail: his voice cracked, and nothing happened.

'Confidence, Fred! Confidence is key!'

'I think Fred just needs a little help,' Grace said, coming to her new friend's rescue.

Fred smiled as she lay beside him and, obviously in her element, started to sing.

As if a switch had been flicked, the worm suddenly lit up. Professor Narly led the boisterous applause as an astonishing arc of colour fanned up and out into the air from the worm's head to its tail.

Shortly after, as each pair of students encouraged their worm to shine, the clearing in the woods was filled with a wondrous display of colourful light.

'Now,' Professor Narly announced, when she had returned the creatures to their wormery, 'I think you're ready to meet another monster.'

Right on cue, an ear-splitting squawk pierced the air. Fred covered his ears, alarmed, and his classmates looked around in fright.

'And I think it's ready to meet you too.'

Chapter Fifteen

The creature swooped like a bird and landed elegantly, silently, like a falling flake of snow.

Though it was only *half*-bird, because the rear of its body – with its tail, muscular haunch and two sharp-clawed paws at the end of its legs – was that of a lion. The beast's vibrant eyes, black pupils sharp against a swirl of yellow, and the pointed hook of its beak gave it a stern, almost disapproving expression. Perfect feathers blanketed its giant, powerful wings, which folded neatly as it rested. *This* must have been what made the tracks they had followed; the talons at the front of its body matched the menace of the claws at its back. Fred knew it was a creature to be wary of, but it was beautiful. He'd never seen anything so majestic.

Professor Narly whispered loud enough to be heard, without startling the beast. 'Does anybody know this creature's name?'

The half-lion, half-eagle's eyes followed the movement of shaking heads.

Fred was clueless, and, although he'd expected them to know, Marvin and Hex seemed to be too. Then again, being outstanding at magic and having knowledge of magical creatures did not by nature go hand in hand, and, as Fred knew, Monster Management was not a subject taught in regular schools. He remembered what Grace had said about kindness and respect for all creatures, and suspected that Hex considered himself above them in the magical hierarchy. If he didn't respect them, why would he bother learning about them? Fred wasn't surprised that Grace knew the answer.

'It's a griffin.'

Professor Narly nodded. 'Go on.'

'Well, they're dangerous creatures – for obvious reasons,' Grace added, as the griffin scraped its claws and snapped its beak at some invisible threat in the air, 'known for guarding treasures – diamonds, gold, priceless possessions. But they're also incredibly loyal. They mate for life, and if you manage to befriend one, they never forget you. Which is also the case if you anger one.'

Fred could see the rest of the class were impressed by Grace's knowledge, and perhaps starting to realize that they'd underestimated her. Judging from the expression on Hex's face, he didn't like someone else giving the answers.

'An excellent summary, Grace.' Professor Narly grinned. 'I was going to ask for a volunteer but I've no—'

'I'll do it!' Hex jumped forward suddenly.

With a piercing shriek, the griffin reared onto its hind legs and flapped its wings. The force of the displaced air knocked the students closest to her off their feet, and Hex stumbled backwards to his place next to Marvin.

'Are you *stupid*, boy?' Professor Narly scolded him. 'You are *not* the person I had in mind.'

Once Professor Narly had succeeded in

calming the beast, she invited Grace to approach. Fred watched admiringly as Grace stepped towards the animal. He knew she was competent, but to him the beast seemed unpredictable, its size and power ferocious …

Grace held the griffin's stare, as instructed, then mirrored its movement, step by single step, until she was close enough to touch it. Fred held his breath.

Ever so slowly, Grace raised her hand to the creature's beak. Fred was impressed with how steady it was …

Without warning, a thunderous **CRACK** whipped the air and sparks shot in all directions, fizzing around at head height. Fred, Grace and a few others spun around in time to glimpse Hex returning his wand to his jacket pocket, but they were powerless as chaos unfolded around them. Startled, the griffin screeched loudly. As the beast thrashed its wings, Grace dived to the ground, evading the spear-like tips of its talons as it took flight.

But another young witch called Maisie turned into the griffin's path at the wrong moment. It picked her up, carrying her a short distance before letting go. Professor Narly, whose attention had been focused on Grace, turned and rapidly fired a spell in the direction of the girl's screams as she dropped towards the bodies taking cover. The cushioning charm came too late. Fred shuddered as Maisie's body thudded onto the ground.

For a sickening moment, Maisie didn't move. Fred glanced at Hex, whose expression was emotionless, then towards Professor Narly, who appeared to be muttering incantations as she crouched next to her student, to relieve or numb her pain, Fred guessed. When the professor, satisfied, glanced up at the rest of her students, Grace understood her appeal for assistance. She kneeled beside Maisie, who had managed to sit up. Grace wrapped one of Maisie's arms around her shoulder and Fred ran to do the same. Together they helped her to stand.

'See that she gets to the Magical Medic in one piece,' the professor sighed, clearly

shaken by events. 'They'll check her over properly.'

As she brought the lesson to an end, Fred and Grace carried Maisie towards the main building and the medic's office. Marvin stood sheepish but speechless; as they passed, he tentatively moved to help, but their glares stopped him in his tracks. Anger raged through Fred; how could Marvin even *consider* being mates with someone like Hex? Suddenly, apologizing didn't seem important at all.

'Nice friend you've made,' Fred said.

Chapter Sixteen

When the Magical Medic had assured Fred and Grace that Maisie would be fine but needed to rest, they had headed to the dining hall for lunch.

Fred had eaten and said little. He and Grace fielded questions from Maisie's concerned friends, who were relieved to hear she'd be okay but frustrated that the medic hadn't let them see her. Fred heard only snippets from the conversations around him, but he could sense everyone's anger at Hex. They seemed no longer in awe of him or his magic — just angry that his arrogance had put one of their friends in danger. For his part, Fred's mind was full. He seethed at the thought of how much worse things could have been if Professor Narly hadn't managed to control the situation so quickly. He hoped at least that Marvin would, finally, have seen what Hex was really like.

Hex appeared untroubled by his conscience. Fred thought perhaps that Marvin looked sheepish and slightly embarrassed in Hex's company, but he couldn't be sure. He noticed Marvin glance in his direction a few times.

Now, as everyone enjoyed the last lesson of the day, Daring Duelling, laughter rang out. Various objects – confetti, sponges, pairs of socks, bubbles, gunge – shot harmlessly across the room as students launched spells at each other. Grace giggled as Fred conjured a pair of comically large, feather-duster-like hands that set about tickling her. She conceded defeat when the sensation became too much to bear, and shook hands with Fred – and the gloves.

Then, at the professor's call to swap partners, Fred felt a tap on his shoulder.

'Is it okay if we …' said Marvin.

Fred nodded.

Without saying more, they practised a few spells, mostly *pretending* to duel, neither of them wanting to make any move that might upset the other.

'I heard Maisie is going to be okay,' Marvin eventually said.

'She'll be fine,' Fred replied shortly.

Marvin nodded. 'I'm sorry that happened.'

'It's not you who should be apologizing, and it's not me who's owed the apology. Why isn't Hex apologizing?'

Marvin sighed. He pretended to fire a spell at Fred, and a harmless mist drifted weakly from his wand.

'If it's any consolation, I don't think he *meant* to hurt anyone.'

'Then why did he do it?'

Marvin shrugged. 'Frustration? He's not used to being second best at something.'

'Or not being the centre of attention?' suggested Fred. 'Not getting his way?'

'Maybe,' Marvin said.

'Why are you even friends with him?' Fred asked.

'Because we hit it off when we saw each other's magic. It was exciting, Fred. I've never met someone my age as brilliant at magic as him, and neither has he.'

'But now it's not *quite* as exciting? He's not *quite* as brilliant as you thought?'

Another awkward silence followed, until Fred found the words he'd been searching for.

'Look, you know I don't like him and –' Fred gritted his teeth – 'I find it hard that *you* like him. But … I'm sorry we fell out, that I've not been as good a friend as you've always been to me. I know I've relied on you too much. I understand that you need to have other friends too. Honestly.'

'Thanks.' Marvin nodded. 'I'm sorry that we argued too.'

Progress of sorts, Fred thought. But when their professor announced that it was time for the competition to begin and they shook hands, their friendship felt far from repaired.

The room soon echoed with cries of triumph and disappointment as the matches unfolded. The competition was fierce, the atmosphere tense again. Victory deserted Fred, who before long was joined on the sidelines by almost everyone else, until there were only four students left duelling.

But the crowd's focus fell on only one of the matches. Those watching on clapped, winced, cheered and recoiled as Marvin and Hex duelled. The fight started fairly, under the professor's careful gaze. But whenever he turned to supervise the other duel, and the longer Marvin withstood Hex's efforts, the less fair and friendly it became.

'HEY! THAT'S DANGEROUS!' Marvin shouted, dodging shards of ice that arrowed towards him from the tip of Hex's wand. Fred, though not surprised, gasped like the rest of the crowd. 'We're not meant to HURT each other, Hex!'

'Don't be *weak*!' Hex grinned, ignoring the crowd's protests, focused only on winning.

Marvin fired a cloud of fog towards
Hex, followed by a powerful sneezing spell,
but Hex evaded both.

Then, quicker than a heartbeat, Hex
fired another spell that was beyond all the
boundaries of friendship. Marvin dived to
avoid Hex's deafening charm – a headful
of torturous noise – as well as the ropes

intended to bind his limbs, but his wand tumbled from his hand. As the referee's focus remained on settling a dispute in the other duel, Marvin was left with only one option.

'*Okay!* You win!' Marvin called. 'Stop!'

Hex wasn't satisfied. He fired another binding spell that Marvin managed to dodge, then raised his arm, taking careful

aim with his wand, determined to get it right *this* time …

'HE SAID, STOP!' The roar grabbed the referee's attention and made Hex turn and hesitate.

Fred charged at Hex: he didn't trust that shouting or a spell would do. But before he could reach Hex, Marvin had scrambled for his wand and, fearing what else Hex might have up his sleeve, conjured a white flag that flapped from the end of it.

'That's it,' the referee announced. 'Duel over!'

The other students muttered to themselves as Hex celebrated. Marvin trudged to a corner of the room and sat alone. Fred sighed at the sight of his best friend looking so lost and lonely. He didn't go over, though. He thought maybe Marvin needed a moment on his own.

The crowd's roar of encouragement pulled Fred's attention to the final duel. He hadn't realized Hex's opponent was Grace – who, to his and everyone's delight, appeared to be *winning*.

Grace twirled, swayed and twisted out of the way of every spell, as if performing a dance that she'd choreographed. Sweat dripped from Hex's brow as he grunted with the effort of trying to overcome her brilliance, ignoring the referee's warning about his increasingly vicious spells. Fred and other onlookers grimaced as Hex's tactics got dirtier, then gasped with astonishment at Grace's response: she matched Hex with an unexpected aggression and ferocity so different to her usual placid demeanour.

Swaying to avoid Hex's suffocating bubble spell, Grace retaliated with a nauseous curse that struck him square in the stomach. His wand fell from his hand, and left him bent

double, unable to continue.

The crowd whooped with delight. Grace didn't celebrate, but winked at Fred, tilting her head in the direction of Marvin. Fred understood, and wandered over to sit down next to his friend.

'Thanks for stepping in. You told me so, Fred.' There was regret in Marvin's eyes. 'I'm sorry that I didn't listen, that I abandoned you.'

Fred ignored the statement.

'I'm sorry that I've been a burden, Marv. I won't be any more, I promise.'

He placed an arm around Marvin's shoulder. 'Friends?' he said.

'No,' Marvin replied. '*Best* friends.'

Chapter Seventeen

'*What* are we going to do for our final performance? It's tonight!'

Marvin and Grace, unable to answer Fred's question, sighed at the same time into their breakfast bowls. Despite sharing their frustration, Fred couldn't hide his grin. Things felt good. He and Marvin had repaired their friendship, and now another was blossoming too, much to his relief – he'd been worried that things as a three might be awkward. But Marvin and Grace had quickly discovered they had plenty in common beyond their fondness for Fred. Their respect for one another's magical talents meant that Fred had soon found himself unable to get a word in as Marvin quizzed Grace on anything and everything to do with magical monsters, and she asked him about the complexities of brewing his memory potion. Fred didn't mind just watching and listening; odd though it felt to have *two* friends by his side, he very much liked that they could all be friends together.

'We've got to think of *something*,' Marvin said. 'We can't miss out on M.A.G.I.C. School when we've had a taste of what it would be like … *Normal* school would be torture.'

Fred looked around the dining hall. Many of their fellow students were busy rehearsing their routines, putting into practice everything they'd learned over the past few days. Someone had transformed a table, which, having discovered that it now had control over its legs, was rampaging around the room and causing chaos.

'If we're *really* going to show what we've learned over the last three days to dazzle and impress the teachers, just like Professor Perdoopa said,' Fred said, 'we've got to stand out. Do something that nobody else would *think* of.'

A sudden squawk interrupted his deliberation as a paper aeroplane transformed mid-air into a beautiful bird. Fred watched as it soared through the open window, never to be seen again – which reminded him of something ...

'I wonder where that griffin went,' he said.

Marvin's eyes lit up.

'That's it! Why don't we try to find the griffin? Imagine how dazzling and impressive *that* would be!'

Fred tried to gauge Grace's reaction. He didn't want to dampen Marvin's enthusiasm, and he'd promised he'd be a more supportive friend, but Marvin's idea was a long shot at best. Judging by her contemplative expression, Grace seemed to consider it a serious option.

'Think about it!' Marvin recognized Fred's uncertainty. 'Tracking and befriending a *griffin*! Including it in our performance somehow ... We'd be showing *loads* of what we learned in Monster Management, at least. It won't have occurred to anyone else ...'

'Probably for good reason,' Fred said. 'It didn't exactly seem like the easiest creature to befriend. And it could be anywhere.

Do you really think we have a chance of finding it?'

'Well, you've got history when it comes to finding monsters,' Marvin reminded Fred. 'And Grace is good with animals – *amazing*, actually. It's not impossible, is it?'

'No, it's not,' Grace said. 'And I've thought of something that might help.'

'See? It's meant to be!' Marvin said cheerily. He addressed Fred's next question before Fred could ask it. 'And if we fail, at least we'll have tried. We've no other ideas. What have we got to lose?'

Limbs? Our lives? Fred thought, the knife-like tips of the griffin's talons flashing through his mind. But he forced a smile.

'It's good to have you back, Marv.'

'There, that should do.' Grace stepped back to admire her handiwork.

Marvin looked himself up and down, then at Fred and Grace's shiny new outfits. The three of them looked as if they were clothed in sunshine.

'I hope you're right, and it's not just a myth that griffins are attracted to gold. I feel like a trophy!'

'If you'd studied the literature, you'd know griffins have always been associated with gold. Their eggs are golden, for a start. Trust me, this is our best bet,' Grace reassured Marvin, as they set off towards the forest.

'Might we end up as the hunted, rather than the hunters?' Fred didn't much fancy being pecked or clawed to death by an enormous eagle-come-lion.

'Quite possibly,' Grace said, 'but isn't that the point? At least it'll mean we find it.'

'That's true,' Fred said, trying to appear casual and calm. He knew their plan was the only one they had – but, really, it was only half a plan.

'Come on, this way.' Grace smiled
cheerfully.

But, after their search had stretched into
the afternoon, even Grace's optimism was
disappearing, along with their chances of
finding the griffin in time – of completing
camp, of earning their M.A.G.I.C. Medals,
of enrolling at M.A.G.I.C. School.

'I'm not sure where else we can go,'
Grace said. 'We need to head back soon,

or we'll miss the ceremony.'

Something disturbed the air above their heads. They looked up, but whatever it was had disappeared.

'Let's look just a *little* longer,' Marvin said.

A faint noise sounded in the distant treetops.

'We need to get closer,' said Fred.

As they hurried deeper into the woodland, the whooshing of branches swaying above them accompanied the rustling of leaves under their feet. Gradually, the noise grew louder, turning from a faint cry to a distinctive squawk, until they were directly beneath it and forced to cover their ears to protect them from the almost-deafening sound …

When they looked up, their hearts sank.

'No!' Marvin cried.

With a frightened squawk, the huge eagle above them departed its perch and flew away into the late-afternoon, sun-streaked sky.

'I was sure it was the griffin too,' Grace said, disappointed.

'Seeing as we can't click-and-go, I think we need to turn back now,' Fred said.

'But what are we going to do for the performance?' Marvin asked.

'Maybe we'll think of something on the way,' Fred replied. He pulled from his pocket a bag of toffees he'd kept in case of an emergency. 'Here. We could do with cheering up, and the chewing is good for thinking, I've found.'

Fred popped a toffee into his mouth, and

set off in the same direction as the others.

As he followed, he made sure to drop one of the sweet wrappers behind him every so often. Just in case.

Their glossy gold wrappers glinted in the sun.

Chapter Eighteen

When they finally took their seats in the back row of the stands, the closing ceremony was well underway. A crowd of young wizards and witches sat facing the stage, each of them anxiously counting down the seconds until they had to perform. The professors assessed proceedings from the front row. After every routine, Professor Perdoopa climbed onstage to shake the performer's hand, before enthusiastically introducing the next act. It was only later, during the official presentation, and once the professors had made their final decisions, that the students would discover if they'd done enough to earn their medal and invitation to M.A.G.I.C. School. The atmosphere was tense, which only increased Fred's own tension.

'When do you think we're up?' Marvin whispered.

Grace picked up the programme from under her seat.

'Luckily, we're last.'

'That gives us more thinking time,' Fred said.

'Hardly,' Marvin sighed, as Uri, a wizard who had only half-reversed his

transformation into a unicorn, trotted off the
stage to the clip-clopping of his back hooves.

'Almost everyone's already performed. *What*
are we going to do?'

They frantically tried to think of something.

'You two could duel?' Fred suggested. 'You were amazing yesterday.'

'But there's *already been* too many. The crowd are getting fed up of them — didn't you hear them boo the last one?' Marvin said. 'We need something special.'

'Right now, we just need *something*,' Grace said.

'Fred, your adventures have been special …' Marvin mused. 'Why don't you tell everyone how they happened, with all the inside details?'

'But that won't involve any magic, or show what I've learned, and — oh dear, we're after the next act!'

Maisie finished her performance with a flourish and bowed; everyone applauded particularly vigorously, pleased to see she'd fully recovered from her injuries. Now, walking towards the centre of the stage to start his routine, was Hex. The applause tailed off. An intrigued, uncertain silence followed.

'Is it just me,' Grace frowned, 'or do you get the feeling the rest of our classmates want him to mess up?'

The boys nodded. Something in the atmosphere had shifted. It now felt hostile, and made Fred – despite his dislike for Hex – feel uncomfortable, as if the will of the crowd to see Hex fail was going to cause something far more serious. The friends forgot about their own performance. All their attention was pulled towards Hex.

Hex clapped his hands and vials of potion appeared in front of him. He whooshed his wand, and the vials moved through the air and into the hands of the professors.

'A thank you for all you've taught us,' Hex said, smiling at the professors, who, seemingly unthinkingly, downed the contents of their vials. Fred couldn't see their expressions, but thought it a reckless thing to do – the potion could be *anything* – before remembering the overwhelming urge that had compelled him do to the same thing just a few days ago, at the start of camp. From the little that Fred could see, there was no obvious effect on the professors or their behaviour, but, based on his usual antics, Fred suspected there was more to Hex's agenda than expressing gratitude. Marvin seemed to agree.

'Suck-up,' he whispered. 'I wonder what else he's up to.'

Onstage, Hex closed his eyes and took several deep breaths. Then he lifted his wand to the fading afternoon sky, and the white clouds above him turned a murky grey, coming together to form a menacing mass. Fred watched as the cloud cast a shadow of darkness across the mesmerized audience. It was powerful magic, an impressive display.

Then a flash of lightning cut through the black and illuminated – for a split second – everything around. Hex flinched as a fork of lightning struck the top of the stage with

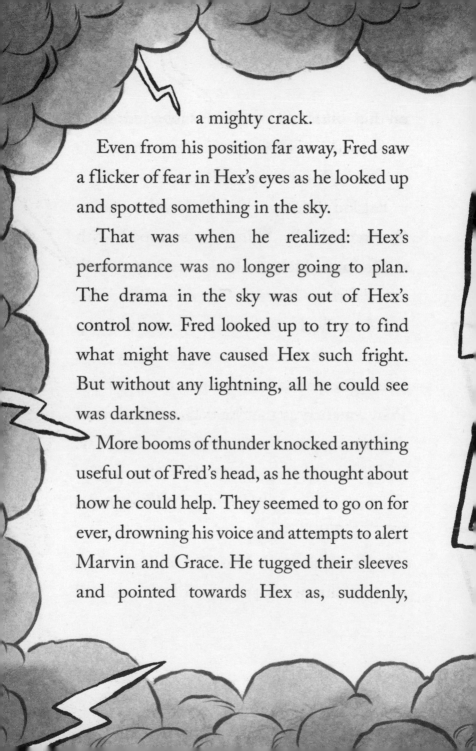

a mighty crack.

Even from his position far away, Fred saw a flicker of fear in Hex's eyes as he looked up and spotted something in the sky.

That was when he realized: Hex's performance was no longer going to plan. The drama in the sky was out of Hex's control now. Fred looked up to try to find what might have caused Hex such fright. But without any lightning, all he could see was darkness.

More booms of thunder knocked anything useful out of Fred's head, as he thought about how he could help. They seemed to go on for ever, drowning his voice and attempts to alert Marvin and Grace. He tugged their sleeves and pointed towards Hex as, suddenly, another blaze of brightness stabbed the sky.

'Something's not right,' he mouthed.

They saw it before they heard it.

Behind the stage, high above, the griffin, fleetingly lit by lightning, swooped with wings outstretched. Then it disappeared, along with the light.

It screeched, and Fred saw the crowd jump again: his fellow students were concerned. Why didn't the professors seem worried? Why wasn't Professor Narly doing anything?

Panic forced Fred out of his seat. The griffin was getting closer. Was it going to attack? Hex scanned the sky, terrified, wand held aloft in defence against the creature that he worried had spotted him, though he didn't know how or why it had appeared now of all times. He fired a warning spell upwards and angry red sparks spiralled into the atmosphere, a lone firework that drowned in the sea of black.

For a moment, everything stilled. There were no more screeches, no more fireworks, no more shards of lightning or thumps of thunder.

The clouds parted and the darkness slowly began to lift. The crowd shielded their eyes against the returning light. Fred squinted up at the sky. Had the griffin gone?

But, when the crowd's eyes had adjusted to the brightness, they let out a gasp of terror. Fred looked up, and his heartbeat doubled. His plan, the trail of golden wrappers, had worked – but in spite of his disagreement with Hex, he hadn't intended *this*.

Silently and invisibly in the darkness, the creature had swooped onto the stage, and it now lurked menacingly behind Hex. The golden wrappers, skewered by its talons, glistened in the last of the afternoon light.

'It's like you said!' Marvin turned to Grace. 'Hex angered the griffin. It recognizes him! It remembers him!'

As Hex slowly turned, aware of a presence behind him, the griffin rose high onto its hind paws and screeched. Hex fell backwards, and cried out as his wand tumbled from his hand and over the edge of the stage …

Some of the audience shrieked and protected their eyes from the gruesome scene that was surely to follow. Yet *still* the professors didn't move.

'Why aren't they *doing* something?' Fred said, but Marvin and Grace were speechless.

The griffin was standing directly over Hex now.

And it was over for Hex …

Chapter Nineteen

Fred shuffled towards the aisle. 'We can't just stand here – it'll rip him to shreds!' Marvin and Grace chased after him as he sprinted towards the stage.

'Hey! Professor Narly!' Fred called. 'Do something!'

But the professors didn't respond.

When he reached them, Fred shivered at their expressions; at the way they had slumped contentedly in their seats; at the way they were smiling and discussing the drama in front of them, as if nothing was amiss.

'What a beautiful griffin,' he heard Professor Narly exclaim.

'A wonderful performance,' Professor Draught said, grinning.

Fred could see the professors' eyes moving, tracking events, but it seemed their brains were failing to compute the messages delivered to them. He wanted to shake them

from their happy stupor, to make them see how serious the situation was. *That* was what Hex's potion had been for! He'd enchanted the professors to believe his performance was perfect. It was a sure way to guarantee he would receive his medal. But it was backfiring spectacularly ...

As Fred reached the stage, he realized they'd been too slow. The griffin's talons were already gripping Hex's torso and it plunged its pointed beak towards the exposed flesh of Hex's neck—

Fred felt Grace's spell *whoosh* past his ear. Hex groaned as it struck him with a brilliant flash, stopping the griffin's beak a hair's breadth from his skin. It jerked back, surprised. Hex was now clothed in gold. Fred could barely comprehend Grace's genius, but hope flickered inside him … until the beast lunged forward once more.

But now, instead of tearing Hex apart, the enormous creature stood upon and smothered his prone body, fiercely guarding its newly acquired treasure. Hex groaned under its weight.

'Grace, that was brilliant,' Fred said, as she and Marvin joined him on the stage. She had bought them some time. 'What now?' As they stood like three gold statues in front of it, the griffin's eyes widened. But it didn't move.

'I don't think it knows whether to leave with Hex or take us too,' Fred said, aware of his heart thumping noisily in his chest, as desperate to escape his body as he was to escape this unpredictable situation in one piece.

Marvin grimaced. 'I thought it would remember you, Grace, but it seems confused – like it doesn't know whether we're friends or enemies. I don't think it recognizes you, covered in gold.'

'Then we've got to win it over,' she said. 'With a gesture of goodwill, of friendship. We need to give it something personal, that it will like.'

'Your glasses!' Marvin suggested. 'They're personal – *and* gold!'

'But I can't see a thing without them ...'

'*Please*,' Hex groaned. '*Help ... me.*' He was struggling to breathe.

Seeing no other option, Grace stepped closer and slid her glasses across the stage. The griffin peered at them. A moment later, it tilted its head at Grace in a gesture of satisfaction, and picked them up in its beak.

'What's going on?' Grace said. 'Did it work?'

'I think so, yes!' Marvin said, as the griffin flapped its wings. 'It's about to go! Wait … *Oh no!*' The beast's talons were still tight around Hex's torso. 'It's going to take Hex with it!'

'Help!' Hex cried, as the griffin lifted him into the air.

The crowd yelped in horror. As the effects of Hex's Pleasing Potion began to wear off, a few of the professors stirred. But, still in a groggy state, they were slow to comprehend what was happening in front of them.

Fred – out of pure instinct, for the first time in his life – reached for his wand.

With a steady hand that belied his nerves, he took aim, and before the beast could fly any higher, he launched his spell. Two objects rose like rockets from his wand and locked onto the griffin's body. The same enormous hands that had tickled Grace into submission set to work on their new target. Within seconds, the griffin was cooing and purring and singing, and its grip on Hex – and Grace's glasses – weakened until, eventually, it loosened completely.

As the beast flew away and Hex fell through the air, Marvin was alert to the

new danger, pointing his wand at Hex. A split second before he crashed to the ground, Marvin transformed Hex's gold outfit so that it inflated around him, cushioning his fall. He landed without so much as a bump, to the relief of everyone watching. Grace's glasses lay on top of him, undamaged.

Fred, Marvin and Grace rushed to check on Hex, who was disorientated and white with shock. Marvin kneeled beside him and made him drink the contents of the tiny vial that he'd pulled from his pocket. Hex grinned contentedly and relaxed as happy memories flooded his mind.

Then Marvin stood up and gave the crowd an enthusiastic thumbs up. They roared with approval. The professors, a little confused as to *exactly* what had happened but impressed nonetheless by the trio's heroics, led the applause.

'Is *that* what you had in mind for our final performance?' Grace chuckled, as she and the others bowed to the audience.

'Not *really*,' Fred and Marvin laughed, 'but it'll do.'

As they made their way back to their seats, to Fred's surprise, Hex grabbed his arm and pulled him aside. He opened and closed his mouth a few times, before finally finding the words he'd been searching for.

'Look, I'm—' Hex looked ashamed. 'Thank you, Fred. And sorry. For everything.'

Fred nodded. He was relieved that

accidentally leading the griffin to Hex hadn't ended in *total* disaster, and felt the guilt it had caused him evaporate. He appreciated Hex's apology – swallowing his pride couldn't have been easy. 'I'm glad you're all right,' he replied.

This was followed by an awkward silence, until Hex, for the first time, smiled at Fred, then muttered a quick 'bye'. As he watched Hex disappear to tend to his wounded pride in private, Fred almost felt sorry for him.

Chapter Twenty

'Now *that* was a closing ceremony!'

The crowd cheered in agreement as Professor Perdoopa addressed them for the final time.

Funny how things turn out, Fred thought to himself. Ironically, Hex's potion had done him and his friends a favour. As well as enabling them to rescue Hex before the adults could intervene, it had worn off at the ideal time; the professors had been able to witness, with their awareness fully restored, the trio's heroics – which had inadvertently demonstrated many of the things they'd learned at camp. Fred saw from their grins that Marvin and Grace were thinking the same thing.

'As a thank you for your efforts,' Professor Perdoopa continued, 'we have a special guest joining us to hand out the M.A.G.I.C. Medals to those of you who have done enough to earn one.'

A wave of whispers rippled through the audience. Professor Perdoopa looked around, as if expecting the VIP to appear next to her, right on cue. As they were nowhere to be seen, she turned back to the crowd.

'First, though, there are a couple of individual awards that, as our guest appears to be running late, it will be *my* pleasure to present.' She peered at the scroll she'd pulled from her robes, then directed a signal to the right of the stage. A goblin appeared from the wings carrying a sparkling trophy in the shape of a wand.

'This will come as little surprise to anyone after her magnificent performance yesterday. She's quiet and kind, but underestimate her at your peril! It is my honour to present the Golden Wand Award to our Champion Dueller – Grace Hannstile!'

Everyone stood to applaud Grace as she accepted her award. Grace, bashful, smiled and blushed, quickly heading back to her seat, eager to celebrate the success of whoever was next.

When Professor Perdoopa announced the winner of the award for Most Masterly Magician at camp, she, along with Fred, cheered louder than anyone else.

'Go, Marvin!'

Marvin looked a little overwhelmed by the warmth of the recognition. He beamed as he shook the professor's hand.

'Well done, Marv,' Fred said, as Marvin returned to his seat clutching a magnificent silver shield engraved with previous winners' names.

'Thanks, Fred. Look, my dad's name's here! He's never mentioned anything!'

'He's modest, like you.' Fred smiled. 'He'll

be really proud – *even more* proud, I mean.'

Marvin nodded without taking his eyes off the shield.

Having handed out the individual awards, Professor Perdoopa was clearly growing increasingly worried that the Very Important Person had decided their invitation was *not* very important after all. Fred thought she might now be inventing awards in order to fill the time and save her embarrassment ...

'So, the next award for the, err ... Hairiest Ears ... goes to – our very own Professor Bush!'

'The award for Most Amusing Impersonation of a Swan goes to ...'

'Next, the Worst Posture Prize is awarded to ... Actually it's you, Gary – so keep that,' she told the hunched-over goblin who was handing out the awards. He looked delighted and uncomfortable all at once.

Then, just as she was about to announce who'd won the prize for perfectly poaching an egg, there was a loud **POP!** and a man appeared onstage.

'Sue, I'm sorry I'm late, and I don't mean to be rude, but it really is all your fault!' His eyes and smile twinkled. 'Your protective enchantments get trickier to negotiate every year, even for me!'

Cheers and squeals rang out, and Merlin turned to face the crowd. 'Hello, everyone!'

Catching Fred's eye, he winked.

Then came the moment everyone had been waiting for.

Fred edged forward in his seat like the rest of his classmates, his ears pricked for the sound of his name. Names were called randomly, not alphabetically, it seemed, which only added to the tension. He whooped with delight when first Grace, and then Marvin, had their name called, but as he watched more students arrive onstage to shake Merlin's hand and collect their medals, Fred's anxiety grew ever worse. He wanted his medal and place at M.A.G.I.C. School more than ever – the thought of missing out, knowing that his two friends would be there without him, was too painful to bear. He crossed his fingers …

'Congratulations, Andy Witherwand!'

Squeezed them tighter …

'Well done, Karma Down!'

More tightly than ever before …

'And finally …' There was a collective groan of disappointment as Fred and the remaining students realized their hopes of being called had virtually vanished. 'Congratulations to …'

Marvin and Grace, standing by the side of stage, stared at Fred with longing in their eyes. He averted his gaze, and bowed his head. He didn't want them to see how upset he was, to spoil their moment of celebration …

'Fred Wandsworth!' Professor Perdoopa announced.

The joyous moments that followed immediately after were a blur to Fred.

But, somehow, legs trembling, he made it
onto the stage.

Later, when the after-party had drawn to a
close, emotional goodbyes were said before
everyone began clicking themselves home.

Under sparkling stars, in the soft light
of the moon, Fred turned his M.A.G.I.C.
Medal over in his hands.

'There's no doubt about it, Fred.' Merlin
had appeared at his side. 'You are a magician
of genius, intrepidness and courage.'

'Yeah.' Fred grinned, though he could
hardly believe it.

'You always have been, of course – but

now it's official! Why don't you put it on?'

Fred hadn't wanted to until now, but, with Merlin's encouragement, he placed the medal round his neck. It felt strangely … *right*.

Fred waved as Marvin and Grace returned from one final lap of the camp's grounds, medals resting proudly on their chests.

'What now?' Marvin asked.

They glanced at one another. No one wanted the night to end, but they knew that it was time to leave.

'Well, it's a bit late for tea …' said Merlin. The others nodded. 'But how does a midnight feast sound?'

'Fitting!' Fred said.

'Perfect!' said Marvin.

'Magical!' Grace beamed.

And the four of them clicked their fingers.

When they arrived at Merlin's house, fittingly, on the stroke of midnight, the feast was waiting for them.

It was perfect.

It was magical.

And that was just how Fred felt.

Have you read all of Fred's magical adventures?

FRED
Wizard in Training

FRED
Wizard in Trouble!
Illustrated by
SHEENA DEMPSEY

FRED
Wizarding Wonder
SIMON PHILIP   Illustrated by SHEENA DEMPSEY

OUT NOW!